For my sister, **Gina**

HODDER CHILDREN'S BOOKS

First published in Great Britain in 2018 by Hodder and Stoughton

Text and illustrations copyright © David Melling, 2018

The moral rights of the author have been asserted.

A CIP record for this book
is available from the British Library.

ISBN: 978 0 340 98970 8

10 9 8 7 6 5 4 3 2 1

Printed and bound in China

Hodder Children's Books
An imprint of Hachette Children's Group
Part of Hodder and Stoughton
Carmelite House
50 Victoria Embankment
London
EC4Y 0DZ

An Hachette UK Company
www.hachette.co.uk
www.hachettechildrens.co.uk

MIX
Paper from
responsible sources
FSC® C104740
FSC
www.fsc.org

Once
Upon
a Bedtime

David Melling

Hodder
Children's
Books

Once upon
a bedtime . . .
a long **yawwwn**
floated down Sleepy Street.

Rabbit was very tired.
It was time to find her friends
and go to sleep.

"C'mon Ellie, bedtime!"
said Rabbit.

"Have you had your bath?" asked Ellie,
SPLISH-SPLASH-SPLOSHING.

"Oh, um . . . not yet."

"We can soon change that!" said Ellie
and filled her trunk with water.

SPLOOOSH!

"Ooh, drippy!" laughed Rabbit. "Ah, look, there's Ollie."

"You look a little wet," said Ollie.

"Yes, I suppose I am!" Rabbit replied.
"Wait, can you hear something?"

It was Monkey and Bird!

"We're singing the Pyjama Lullaby," said Monkey.
"Do you want to join in?"

"You'll need your pyjamas!"
sang Bird.

"**Tra**-la-la! Py**ja**ma-**ma**-la! Let's all **sing**-a lulla**lalala**-by!"

"Is anyone sleepy yet?" asked Monkey.

"Not yet," said Rabbit. "I'm wondering
who that long spiky tail belongs to . . ."

"It's me!" said Crocodile, smiling his wide crocodile smile!

"Of course," said Rabbit. "We nearly forgot to clean our teeth!"

Brush,

brush,

brush,

mmm – that's better!

"Bedtime at last," smiled Rabbit, sleepily.

"Don't forget your cuddlies!"

They all bustled into bed, ready for a story.

"Once upon a **bedtime** there was a very tired …"

SNIFFLE. SNUFFLE. **SNOZ!**

"Who said that?" asked Rabbit.

"Wasn't me," they all gulped.
"It's coming from under the bed!"

"Everybody hide!"
they cried.

And they did.
(Some were better at hiding than others.)

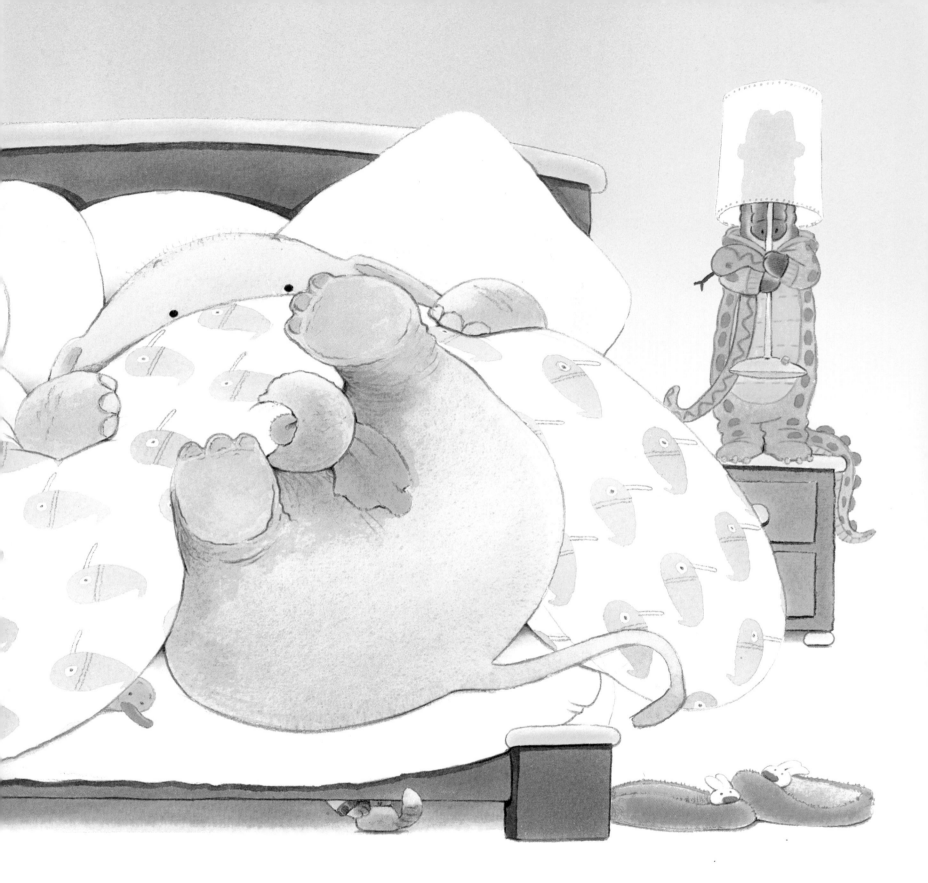

"But wait . . . where's Rabbit?" whispered Ellie.

Rabbit has hidden under the bed by mistake.
Silly Rabbit!

She found herself looking at a . . . **Thing!**

The **Thing** looked sad.

"Who are you?" asked Rabbit.

"What's the matter?"

"I'm a thing without a cuddly," it said
and **sniffled, snuffled** and **snozzled**
some more.

Everyone felt sorry for Thing
(and a little silly for hiding).

**"You can share one of ours,
if you like,"** they all said.

"So many to choose from!" whispered Thing shyly.

"This one . . .
I like this one,"
Thing said and hugged
the cuddly tight with its
long furry arms.

Everyone climbed back into bed again,
ready for a story, but the bright moon was
just a little too bright, even with the curtains closed.

"I'll switch it off!" said Thing
and stretched a long furry arm

up and **up** until it reached the moon.

C-L-I-C-K

"That's just right for reading," said Rabbit.

"And sleeping," yawned the others.
"Now, where were we?"

"Once upon
a **bedtime** . . .

... and they all slept **happily ever after**."

ZZZZZZZZZZZ

The End